Special thanks to Mandy Archer.

For Eti Cleeve, a little girl with
lots of fairy sparkle!

ORCHARD BOOKS
338 Euston Road, London NW1 3BH
Orchard Books Australia
Level 17/207 Kent Street, Sydney, NSW 2000

A Paperback Original

First published in 2010 by Orchard Books.

© 2010 Rainbow Magic Limited.
A HIT Entertainment company. Rainbow Magic
is a trademark of Rainbow Magic Limited.
Reg. U.S. Pat. & Tm. Off. And other countries.

Illustrations © Orchard Books 2010

A CIP catalogue record for this book is available
from the British Library.

ISBN 978 1 40830 812 7

3 5 7 9 10 8 6 4 2

Printed in Great Britain

The paper and board used in this paperback are natural recyclable
products made from wood grown in sustainable forests. The
manufacturing processes conform to the environmental regulations
of the country of origin.

Orchard Books is a division of Hachette Children's Books,
an Hachette UK company

www.hachette.co.uk

Katie
and the Missing Kitten

Choose your own Magic

by Daisy Meadows

ORCHARD BOOKS

www.rainbowmagic.co.uk

Pets choose their owners, fairies say,
Why has my snowgoose gone away?
The ice-white bird has flown its nest,
Yet I was the one who loved it best.

Lightning flash and thunder clap!
I'll set a cruel Pet Keeper trap.
You can't thwart me, not this time,
Fairy friends won't stop my crime.

Kittens play and kittens sleep,
Into Fairyland I'll creep,
Katie's going to lose her friend,
How will Shimmer's story end?

Katie the Kitten Fairy
needs your help!

Can you be the special friend
who helps Katie and Shimmer in their
time of need...?All you have to do is believe
in magic, open the pages of this book and
choose your own path through the story
to rescue poor Shimmer from wicked
Jack Frost! There are lots of different
routes you can take and plenty of fairy
friends to help you along the way!

1

You're drifting off to sleep one chilly night, when you are roused by a strange crying noise coming from the street below. As you sit up and pull back the curtain, an enchanted silvery light streams into your bedroom. The moonbeams are sparkling so prettily, your heart flutters with excitement!

Outside, you can see a little tortoiseshell cat mewing up to the stars. Soon the cat's meows are joined by dozens of other local kitties, each caterwauling as loudly as they can. You hop out of bed, determined to find out what's wrong.

As you open the window, something cold makes your nose twitch – a beautiful snowflake! You hold the flake carefully on your finger so that you can study its delicate diamond-shaped points, astonished that it isn't melting. The sight makes your heart leap! Could magic be in the air? A fine dusting of snow is silently settling, even though winter is still months away.

Suddenly the little cat stops meowing.

"What is that?" you gasp. A strange silvery glow

⭐ Turn to the next page! ⭐

is gliding past the kitten, up towards your window.
As it gets closer, the glow turns into a shimmer
of fairy sparkles, with a smiling fairy fluttering in
the centre!

"Hello!" smiles Crystal the Snow Fairy. "Sorry
to wake you!"

Crystal is wearing a fur-trimmed blue dress
and a tiny pair of matching boots. An exquisite
snowflake necklace shimmers at her neck. You
peep your head out of the window and feel cold,
frosty air whistling around you. Crystal's outfit is
perfect for a night like this!

Crystal smiles shyly, then comes to sit on your
hand. She manages to give your little finger a
friendly squeeze, but the poor fairy looks tired out.

"I've travelled all the way from Fairyland," she
explains. "My friends are in desperate need of
your help."

You would love to help the Rainbow Magic
fairies, but wonder what you can do on such an
icy evening?

* If you decide to find your dressing gown and wait
for Crystal's instructions, go to 26.

* If you think it's best to set your alarm for a dawn
start and promise to help first thing, go to 47.

"Magical animals are very special, aren't they?" you whisper to Katie. "Let's go and see her."

You flit closer to Belle. As you approach, Katie reminds you that Belle has special powers that help every human and fairy to be compassionate and kind.

"Hello," you say shyly. "We're looking for Katie's kitten, Shimmer."

Belle nods her head gracefully and polishes a circle of ice with her feathers until it shines like a mirror. Suddenly, a picture forms in the ice! You see Jack Frost sitting on his spiky blue throne. A fairy hovers unseen in the background, a look of concern on her face. The Ice Lord is very upset about the loss of his beloved pet snowgeese! Katie tells you that the flock of geese can usually be found swimming on this very pond. You feel very sorry for the lonely ruler. He must be feeling just as sad as poor Katie.

Suddenly, a whirl of fairy magic spins you both around, and you, Katie and Belle find yourselves in Jack Frost's Ice Castle!

* If you decide to hide behind the crystal throne so that you can keep spying on Jack Frost, go to 6.

* If you decide to find Sophia the Snow Swan Fairy, go to 28.

3

Your heart misses a beat, but something urges you to flutter over the aquamarine waters of the Fairyland Palace pool. You find yourself hovering above the deep end.

Now you can see the stranger much more clearly. He is stretched out on a lilo, his face completely hidden by shades and a straw sunhat. No wonder Samantha was worried – this is clearly no fairy!

You flutter straight back to your friends.

"It's definitely one of Jack Frost's goblins," you tell Katie. "It must be the same one who left footprints in your toadstool last night."

The silly creature is obviously trying to go undercover, but he can't hide his big feet and pointy nose!

Samantha shakes her head and pulls a towel around her. "The naughty creature has been hogging the pool all morning!"

You think that the goblin must be involved in Jack Frost's plot, but Katie shakes her head.

"Surely anybody mean enough to steal Shimmer would take him far away from the safety of Fairyland," she reasons, her little wings drooping with worry.

* If you find the courage to disturb the floating goblin's daydreams, go to 7.

* If you choose to fly on until you discover a more likely hiding place for Shimmer the kitten, go to 8.

4

While the rest of the Pet Keeper Fairies wait at home in case Shimmer returns, you and Katie follow the trail of muddy goblin footprints.

"Look," Katie gasps. "They're going straight out of the front door!"

The prints lead you out of the toadstool, across the garden, and then up into the hills of Fairyland. You flutter from footprint to footprint, but Katie wrinkles her nose in surprise when the footprints curve into a fairy forest and out the other side.

"This path takes us to the Fairyland Palace," she says. "Why would a catnapping goblin go there?"

In a few moments you find yourselves approaching a beautiful outdoor swimming pool at the back of the palace.

"Katie," you say, staring at the ground. "The footprints have stopped!"

As you get closer, Samantha the Swimming Fairy runs out from the changing hut. She is pointing to the pool. You crane your neck and see a person floating on a lilo, their face covered by a large straw sunhat.

* If you choose to flutter over the water, go to 3.
* If you'd prefer to ask Samantha what the matter is, go to 19.

5

King Oberon and Queen Titania lead you to the throne room. Before you can speak, the king mutters a spell, summoning Jack Frost to his presence.

A vision of the Ice Lord appears on a giant sheet of polished ice that spins in the air above you all.

"You have caused a lot of trouble," says the queen. "You had no right to take Shimmer!"

Jack Frost scowls. "It's not fair that Katie has a pet if mine has gone away!"

You step forward and present the Ice Lord with a white feather from his favourite goose. The king explains that this is proof that the flock will return to Jack Frost when the nesting season is over.

"You must go now!" commands King Oberon. He clicks his fingers and the ice sheet disappears.

Now that Fairyland is safe again, the Pet Keeper Fairies invite you to a party to say thank you!

You flutter off to join them for an afternoon of games, dancing and lots of magical pet fun!

The End

You and Katie tumble behind Jack Frost's throne. Belle perches next to you. Suddenly a little hand squeezes your arm.

"Hello!" whispers Sophia the Snow Swan Fairy.

She tells you that she and Belle came here because Jack Frost is also in need of some kindness at the moment. Just then, you hear Jack Frost's shouts echo round the chamber.

"Why should Katie the Kitten Fairy have her pet if I can't have mine?" he roars. "I loved my snowgeese too! I'll keep stealing the Pet Keeper's friends, then they'll understand how *I* feel!"

Sophia explains that a flock of geese used to swim on the Ice Lord's frozen pond. "One day the birds left and flew south. Even Jack Frost's favourite goose has left him!"

You realise that you need to find the snowgeese fast! "Unless his pets are returned, he's sure to cause even more trouble!" you gasp.

You and Katie hug Sophia and Belle farewell and then set off again. You know the birds have gone south, so you set your sights on the sunny climes of Fairyland and beyond. After fluttering for a little while, the pink turrets and domes of the Fairyland Palace loom before you.

* If you decide to flutter over the enchanted building as swiftly as you can, go to 8.
* If you choose to land on the terraces at the back of the king and queen's residence, go to 13.

You reach for Katie's hand and then flutter over
the palace swimming pool. As you fly, a terrible
wailing sound echoes in your ears, drowning
out the beautiful music being played in the
rose garden by the Music Fairies and the frog
orchestra.

Samantha the Swimming Fairy tiptoes up and
down the side of the pool.

"I wish that stranger would go away," she sighs,
pointing to the glittering water. "He doesn't look
very friendly."

You wait for a moment, but the figure doesn't
move. He drifts lazily on a lilo, hogging the water.
His face stays hidden under a sunhat, but his
gangly body almost takes up the entire pool.

In an act of courage, you swoop down and lift
the sunhat off the intruder's head. The sneaky
goblin underneath wakes up with a splutter!

With a cry of "Oi!", the goblin lurches towards
you, before falling off the lilo with a mighty
splash. While he flounders in the water, you peer
into the hat.

"Oh, Katie!" you cry. "Look who's inside!"

Katie giggles with delight as Shimmer trots up to
her, delighted to be free from the goblin's clutches.
The tiny cat had been caterwauling to the music

coming from the rose garden, but the sunhat had kept her hidden from sight!

Shimmer meows urgently to her best friend while Katie interprets. It seems that Jack Frost told the goblin to hide the little cat near the water, as this was the last place that anyone would expect to find her.

At the side of the pool, Samantha the Swimming Fairy claps and cheers, then touches the goblin with her wand. The naughty catnapper howls with displeasure as he finds himself being lifted out of the water and dumped in a heap on the edge of the pool.

"Pesky fairies!" he bellows, shaking his fist.

As he runs away, you give Shimmer a lovely cuddle.

"It's wonderful to have you back!" you beam. "Now we need to think what we can do to stop Jack Frost striking again."

* If you decide to continue your search for Jack Frost's snowgeese, go to 14.

* If you'd rather speak to the rest of the Pet Keeper Fairies, go to 21.

You follow Katie up higher and higher, until you get the best view of the land beneath you. After a while you find yourselves fluttering over the laundry at the back of the Fairyland Palace. You can make out Kylie the Carnival Fairy washing her costumes and Bethany the Ballet Fairy sewing sequins onto her favourite tutu.

You can't help but laugh when you spot Flora the Fancy Dress Fairy pushing a trolley full of outfits with a funny fluffy hat perched on the top.

"I wonder what costume that's for?" you giggle.

Katie the Kitten Fairy suddenly gasps in astonishment. It is only when you glide down to the trolley that you realise that the hat is actually Shimmer curled up asleep!

"I can't believe it's you!" beams Katie, scooping Shimmer up into her arms and covering her with kisses! The tiny cat stretches and purrs, thrilled to be reunited with the Pet Keeper Fairy after her tiring night.

You listen intently as the cat mews to you both, explaining how she managed to escape the goblin who trapped her before she was smuggled out of Fairyland. Lost and frightened, the kitten had curled up to sleep in the cosiest place she could find – Flora's washing.

Katie claps her hands with delight. "Flora!" she calls, grinning at the Fancy Dress Fairy. "Please tell King Oberon and Queen Titania that Shimmer is safe."

While Flora flutters away, you try to decide what to do next. Unless Jack Frost's own pets are found, there is every chance that he could strike again!

* If you ask Katie to send a message to a fairy in the south, go to 20.
* If you flutter up to the palace rooftop and ask the Weather Fairies if they have spotted Jack Frost's snowgeese, go to 39.

You reach as far forward as you can, desperate to catch Katie's delicate wand before it falls into goblin hands.

"I-I can't do it!" you wail, unable to stretch quite far enough.

"Return!" cries Katie, her eyes focussed on the golden rod. Before the wand is lost, it somehow floats back into your hands!

The goblins are so astounded by this magic feat that they let go of you, giving you just enough time to wave the wand over their heads.

"Back you go!" you shout.

All at once the band of naughty goblins are sent marching back to the castle. They grumble and shout, but resisting is impossible. They're under the spell of Rainbow Magic!

When they've disappeared, you and Katie hug tightly.

Suddenly, a little fairy tiptoes out from beside the pond. She is wearing a sparkly cardigan and skinny jeans. A tiny cat is tucked under her arm.

"Hello!" she beams. "I'm Lara the Black Cat Fairy."

* If you choose to ask Lara for news of Shimmer, go to 17.

* If you'd rather find a safe hiding place first in case the goblins come back, go to 32.

Jack Frost is stomping around when the throne room door opens. The king and queen smile as Summer the Holiday Fairy flutters in.

"Not another fairy!" scowls Jack Frost. "What does she want with me?"

Summer approaches the Ice Lord. "I have come to tell you that your geese are nesting on Rainspell Island! Listen to this."

She passes round a pink shell. When you hold it to your ear you hear the contented chirrups of the snowgeese and their young! Jack Frost is delighted.

"If you apologise for stealing Shimmer, you can take the shell home," announces King Oberon.

The Ice Lord grudgingly says sorry and sweeps out of the door. "What a relief!" you smile.

It's nearly time for you to go home too, but before you leave, Katie and her friends present you with a gold necklace inlaid with a tiny kitten charm. It's a true thank you – not just for saving Shimmer, but for proving that a little person can do anything when they have a kind heart!

The End

Within seconds you find yourself being magically transported to the Ice Lord's castle. You flit from door to door until you finally discover Jack Frost sitting glumly on the throne.

"What are you doing here?" he shouts. Then he tries to strike you with an ice bolt!

"Wait!" you cry, holding out the white goose feather.

"This feather comes from your favourite snow goose," you say. "It proves that your flock is well."

Jack Frost snatches the feather and listens as you explain that the birds are nesting in the south for the summer. When they come back, there'll be a gaggle of snowgoslings in tow!

Jack Frost throws open the windows of his chamber and points his wand at the frozen pond.

"I'm going to need a bigger pond!" he cries happily, casting a spell to double its size.

You quietly slip out of the castle. "Now I must go home," you whisper sadly.

In bed that evening, a surprise is waiting for you. Under your pillow you discover a tiny silk bag filled to the brim with golden fairy dust, and a thank-you card from Katie!

You drift off to sleep with a smile on your face – from now on Fairyland is just a sprinkling away!

The End

King Oberon and Queen Titania make their way
to the royal kitchens to welcome Shimmer. They
each stroke the little kitten, thrilled to see her
again.

On their instruction, you nudge the goblin with
a wooden spoon so that he stands up to face Their
Fairy Highnesses!

"Why is your master filled with such fury?" asks
King Oberon.

The goblin pulls a face, then explains that the
Ice Lord is livid that his own pets have left him.
Now that he's doomed to live alone forever in his
Ice Castle, Jack Frost has been in a terrible mood.

King Oberon looks at his queen and laughs.
"The birds haven't left the kingdom forever! They
are just doing what comes naturally."

The queen patiently explains that the birds
must fly south every winter so that they can find
somewhere warm to hatch their babies.

The goblin shrugs, fiddling nervously with a
soft leather purse that is fastened to his purple
loincloth. When pressed, the creature pulls out
a shard of solid ice.

"Jack Frost uses it to check on me," he grumbles.
"When I rub it, the boss appears in the ice."

* If the king decides to summon the Ice Lord himself, go to 5.
* If you decide to give Jack Frost a gift that will help him
  understand, go to 27.

Your quest to track down Jack Frost's snowgeese sees you fluttering across Fairyland and directly over the back of the royal palace. It is only there that you realise how tired your little wings are. You pause in midair to get your breath back.

"Oh, look!" says Katie, giving you a friendly nudge. "There's Bertram!"

You wave down to the king's frog footman, then fly past the kitchens where lunch is being prepared.

Bertram's helpers make a stunning sight as they proceed to the royal ballroom with silver platters held high above their heads. As another palace servant walks beneath you carrying a platter for their royal highnesses, a loud mewing suddenly catches your attention.

You swoop down and lift the silver lid off the tray to find Shimmer underneath, tucking into a fillet of salmon! The kitten is thrilled to see you both – purring with delight as soon as she spots Katie.

"What happened, Shimmer?" asks the overjoyed Kitten Fairy.

"Where have you been?"

The little cat twitches her cute pink nose and suddenly transforms into goblin form, acting out how she was snatched in the middle of the night. It seems that the goblin had been trying to find a hiding place for the tiny hostage when he sneaked past the palace kitchens. The smell of all the scrummy fairy food was so delicious, he crept inside to see what he could steal.

The kitten leads you and Katie into the pantry. The greedy goblin is still asleep under a table in the corner!

"Get up!" says Katie, prodding him with her wand.

"Eh?" mutters the goblin, waking up with a burp!

"You're in big trouble!" you cry. "Stay there or we'll tell Jack Frost what you've been up to!"

The goblin slumps sulkily on the floor.

"That showed him," giggles Katie.

"I don't think we can relax just yet," you say. "Unless Jack Frost gets his snowgeese back, he's sure to cause trouble all over again!"

* If you decide to question the goblin about Jack Frost's plans, go to 12.

* If you choose to go and ask the Weather Fairies if they have seen the missing birds, go to 39.

You press on with your search for the missing snowgeese, fluttering past the royal throne room. Katie keeps Shimmer firmly tucked under her arm!

Suddenly you both stop in your tracks. Jack Frost and a legion of goblins are hurtling towards the palace on a fast-moving bridge of ice!

"Come on!" you cry, grasping Katie's arm. "Let's alert the king and queen!"

You head for the royal chamber, but King Oberon and Queen Titania have already seen the angry visitor. When Jack Frost finally bursts through the doors, Their Royal Highnesses command him to mind his manners.

"Why should I listen to you fairy folk?" snarls Jack Frost. "You're all a bunch of goody-goodies!"

The goblins cheer behind him, but the Ice Lord lifts a bony hand to silence them. He seems to sense that the king and queen have something important to show him.

* If you decide to wait for King Oberon to summon Summer the Holiday Fairy, go to 10.

* If you decide to help Their Majesties present Jack Frost with a special gift, go to 27.

You flutter hand-in-hand with Katie and her friends towards the Fairyland Palace.

When you finally land in front of the royal residence, a frog footman opens the doors and courteously ushers you all inside.

You flutter through the corridors until the footman stops at the door of the throne room.

"Welcome, friends!" commands a regal voice.

Inside, King Oberon and Queen Titania are sitting majestically on golden thrones. You all curtsey before Their Royal Highnesses.

Katie the Kitten Fairy flutters forward and tells the king and queen about Jack Frost's snowgeese.

"I'm afraid that the Ice Lord is consumed with jealousy," Queen Titania frowns sadly.

King Oberon reminds you all of the importance of Shimmer's special magic.

"Katie's kitten has the power to help lost and homeless cats find safe homes," he says. "She must be found immediately."

"I'll help Katie lead the search," you say bravely.

Queen Titania's face breaks into a smile.

"Thank you," she says. "But remember that Jack Frost is cunning. Start by looking in all of the places where you'd least expect to find a kitten."

* If you ask Katie to help you search the palace, go to 18.

* If you decide to thank Their Majesties and continue on your way, go to 35.

You flutter down the stairs and creep into the palace throne room. Jack Frost is filled with such fury you can hardly bear to look at him!

"This behaviour will not do!" booms the king, striking his staff on the floor to demand silence.

Although he ought to punish Jack Frost for his terrible behaviour, the king says he has some sympathy for the loss of his beloved pets. Jack Frost first scowls and then smiles when Their Majesties explain that the birds haven't deserted him at all.

"Geese need to migrate to a warm place every year so that they can lay their eggs," smiles Queen Titania.

"But I miss them!" replies Jack Frost.

"Go back to your kingdom and wait for the flock to return," commands the king. "If you steal any more pets, I will not be so forgiving."

In an act of pure kindness the king says Sophia the Snow Swan Fairy has agreed to let Belle visit him regularly until the birds return.

The Ice Lord is satisfied at last. He gathers his cloak and sweeps out of the door.

"I must go too," you say.

Before you can hug your new fairy friends goodbye you are treated to a thank-you cuddle from Shimmer – the cutest kitten in the world!

The End

Lara explains that she followed you here as soon as she heard the news of Shimmer's disappearance. She thought you'd need some good luck in these lonely parts!

"Have you heard anything about my kitten?" asks Katie.

Lara shakes her head and points to the frozen pond.

"This pond is normally full of happy snowgeese," she begins. "Jack Frost loves them dearly. But the entire flock has flown away – they just got up one morning and headed south! Even Jack Frost's favourite goose has decided to leave home."

Katie bites her lip. "Jack Frost must have decided to steal Shimmer out of spite! Let's head up into the skies and see if we can spot anything."

You suggest flying south to search for the missing snowgeese. "If we can find Jack Frost's pets," you suggest, "surely he'll give up Shimmer in return?"

* If you decide to follow Katie up into the frosty skies, go to 8.
* If you decide to lead the way south to Fairyland, go to 13.

18

You decide to explore the Fairyland Palace. Could Shimmer be hiding right under your noses? A cruel joke like this would be sure to give the Ice Lord some satisfaction after losing his snowgeese.

As you flutter above the formal gardens, you spot legions of loyal frog footmen searching every turret, reception room and bedchamber for a sign of the little cat.

"It's no good," you say eventually. "If Shimmer was here, someone would have found her!"

Poor Katie's face falls and a tiny tear drops to the ground. You flutter over to give her a hug but a strange caterwauling makes you pause.

Below you, the Music Fairies are sitting in a beautiful rose garden, preparing to play with the frog orchestra. Victoria the Violin Fairy is performing a solo, but her playing is accompanied by a terrible wailing noise that is totally out of tune! Victoria doesn't understand what is wrong with her instrument.

* If you try and stay focussed on your quest to find Katie's beloved kitten, go to 7.
* If you think that you should stop to help Victoria, go to 30.

You link arms with Katie and then hurry over to find out what's bothering Samantha. The little fairy points to the middle of the pool, which is almost completely filled by a large character lounging on a lilo. It is wearing an enormous pair of flippers and its face is completely hidden by a giant sunhat.

You, Samantha and Katie flutter silently behind one of the palace's bright stripy changing huts, so that you can exchange whispers.

"That stranger has been here all morning," says Samantha in a hushed voice. "Every time I call out to them they just pull their sunhat further down over their face."

Knowing that he or she is much too large to be a fairy, you and Katie swap glances. It is clear to you both that there is a goblin in the pool!

"He must be wearing the flippers to hide his big green toes," says the Kitten Fairy.

You agree. "I'll bet it's the same meanie who trespassed in your toadstool last night."

But Katie still cannot believe that this mischief-maker is the one you're after.

"Shimmer can't stand water," she frowns. "Why would a catnapper bring her here?"

* If you decide to surprise the goblin in the pool, go to 7.

* If you ask Samantha to keep an eye on the stranger and then fly on, go to 30.

Katie pauses for a
moment to rack her
brains. Suddenly she
waves her wand, and a scroll
of parchment appears with the
label "Fairy Telegram" printed on it.

"I know just the fairy!" she grins, her eyes
bright with excitement.

As she dictates the telegram out loud, the words
magically appear on the scroll! Katie quickly
sends the message to Summer the Holiday Fairy,
a dear friend who is holidaying on Rainspell
Island.

A reply appears in seconds, along with a white
goose feather that tumbles into your hands!

Katie happily plucks the telegram out of the air.
Summer confirms that the snowgeese have been
nesting near the south beach on Rainspell, away
from the cold winter days outside Jack Frost's Ice
Castle. When their babies are big and strong, Jack
Frost's beloved pets will return to him.

"We must find the Ice Lord and share this news,"
you cry. "We can't wait another second!"

Katie and Shimmer call for the rest of the
Pet Keeper Fairies, then whisper a powerful
transportation spell.

* If you choose to whirl boldly into Jack Frost's Ice
  Castle, go to 11.
* If you'd prefer to ask Katie to join you on this one last
  journey, go to 22.

You, Katie and Shimmer burst into the palace throne room, where the king and queen are talking to the Pet Keeper Fairies.

"Hooray!" cheers Lauren the Puppy Fairy. "We've been so worried."

Sunny the puppy performs a midair somersault before trotting up to lick Shimmer's nose!

You explain your concern about Jack Frost's snowgeese to the king and queen.

King Oberon bangs his staff on the golden tiles beneath his feet. Suddenly you can see and hear the sights and sounds of the seaside! Up above your heads, you see the snowgeese flying in the sky, accompanied by some cute baby geese!

The king smiles. "Summer the Holiday Fairy tells us that the geese are nesting on Rainspell Island. They will return to the Ice Castle soon."

You grin at Katie, thrilled to hear the news!

"Let me in NOW!" a voice shouts.

Oh no! Jack Frost is at the door and he's spitting with rage!

* If you decide to wait for King Oberon to call Summer the Holiday Fairy, go to 10.

* If you decide to summon all your courage and explain to Jack Frost what has happened to his pets, go to 36.

You take Katie's tiny hands and ask her if she is brave enough to come with you. Shimmer's green eyes gleam and the plucky little cat shines with amber sparkles. You gasp as she suddenly grows to tiger-size!

"Count me in!" Katie laughs, catching Shimmer as she returns to fairy-size!

The rest of the Pet Keeper Fairies touch wands and repeat their transportation spell. In a trice, you find yourselves fluttering along the gloomy corridors of the Ice Castle. At last you spot Jack Frost outside in the snow. The lonely character is sitting beside his frozen pond, attended by his goblin servants.

"Poor thing," sighs Katie, darting closer.

Shimmer gambols towards the goblins too, leaving a trail of sparkles in the icy air. As soon as he spots the kitten, Jack Frost leaps furiously to his feet.

"Grab that cat!" he bellows to his goblins.

Luckily the Ice Lord's henchmen are hopeless. The tiny pet expertly dodges from left to right. You and Katie flutter past.

"The geese will only be allowed to come back here if you promise never to steal another animal again," you warn. You hand him the white feather, proof that his precious geese are safe.

Jack Frost moodily nods his head, but you are heartened to see that he calls off his goblins. You, Katie and Shimmer slip into the icicle forest, keen to get away before the cold-hearted ruler changes his mind.

With a wave of Katie's wand you are back in Fairyland, in the middle of the biggest celebration you have ever seen! The Party Fairies rush forward with plates of delicate fairy food, beautiful music fills the air and multicoloured fountains of glitter spring up magically.

"Come with me," beams the Kitten Fairy. She flutters her peachy wings and leads you up to the Fairyland Palace balcony. Queen Titania and King Oberon bow and point towards the starry sky. There, above the fairy crowds and toadstool houses, is your name lit up in fireworks!

It's been a day filled with wonder and magic – an adventure you'll never, ever forget!

The End

You stop and take a closer look around the pen. You pick up the smallest white kitten and it purrs, then leaps out of your arms, darting after a ball of wool that has rolled out from behind the basket.

As the kittens bat the wool you see that a tiny fairy is tugging the end of the thread!

"I've found you at last!" she cries. "I'm Katie the Kitten Fairy. I'm so pleased to meet you!"

"Are these your kittens?" you ask shyly.

Katie shakes her head, her face filling with worry. "My kitten is called Shimmer and I think she's been stolen!"

"Who took her?" you ask.

Katie shivers. "I'm sure it was Jack Frost."

Katie explains that Shimmer controls the magic that helps lost and lonely kittens and cats to find good homes.

"I'll help you find her," you promise. "Together, we'll get Shimmer back!"

Katie claps her hands in gratitude, then gives you some special instructions.

* If Katie tells you to peep your head through the cat flap at the end of the room, go to 24.
* If you are asked to stand as still as a statue, go to 33.

Katie's face brightens.

"Can you see that cat flap?" she asks, pointing her wand towards a door at the end of the room. "Please push it open a little."

You rush over and peep through the flap. Beyond the door you can see a vivid rainbow arching across the fields at the back of the rescue centre.

"The back door is locked," explains Katie. "We'll have to get out through there."

Your tummy fills with butterflies as you realise that there is only one way to fit through the cat flap!

Katie gently touches you with her wand. In seconds you have shrunk to fairy-size, a pair of filmy wings fluttering on your back.

"They feel tickly," you giggle.

You can't resist looping round the room. As you flutter, a trail of fairy dust glitters behind you.

When you're ready, you and Katie give the cat flap a big push. Katie goes first, slipping through the gap at just the right moment.

You follow her, flying towards the cat flap as fast as you can, and make it through just in time! Now you're outside in the fresh air, feeling the warm glow of sunshine on your wings.

* If you decide to flutter up to the rainbow you can see arching above you, go to 25.

* If you choose to take Katie's hand and ask her to lead you to Fairyland, go to 52.

You spiral up and up into the morning sky, feeling wisps of cloud brush your face. Mirrored raindrops glisten on your wings. Up above, a stunning rainbow is filling the sky, glittering with magic for all to see.

Katie takes your hand and leads you right to the top. At the crest of the rainbow, the brilliant colours reflect beautifully on the Kitten Fairy's delicate wings.

"Do you know that rainbows are actually magical slides?" she asks. "Fairies and their visitors can ride on them whenever they want to go to Fairyland."

Katie sprinkles golden fairy dust over you, then suddenly leaps off the side of the rainbow. You gasp in surprise when she sticks her head out from underneath and reaches for your hand.

"Come on," she says. "It's quite safe."

"What's on this side of the rainbow?" you ask, unable to resist a shiver. The underside still glows with colour, but it also feels shadowy and mysterious.

Katie pauses, then lowers her voice.

"At the other side of the rainbow's arch lies Jack Frost's ice kingdom," she replies. "We need to find out if Shimmer's been taken there."

You put your little hands on the rainbow and push yourselves off. You slide beneath the bands of colour, covering miles in the blink of an eye.

"Oh!" you cry, finding yourself suddenly surrounded by white light. "Are we here?"

You've both tumbled into a drift of freshly laid snow!

* If you decide to clamber out of the snowdrift and then head north, go to 41.

* If you think it's wiser to flutter towards the icicle forest over to the east, go to 50.

You run to your wardrobe and pull out your
dressing gown and slippers, before opening the
window wide enough for Crystal to flutter inside.
As she flies, a fine dusting of silver snowflakes
sparkle and glow, lighting up the bedroom
around her!

"Thank you so much," says Crystal. "You are
a true fairy friend."

The little fairy perches on the edge of the
drinking glass you keep next to your bed,
freezing the water with a touch
of her delicate wand.

You lean down and
touch the ice with your
finger, then pull back
when you realise that a
picture is forming on the
surface!

"Are they the Pet Keeper
Fairies?" you whisper,
pointing to seven miniature
figures moving within the ice. The friends are
fluttering left and right in a panic, as if they have
lost something very important. One of them, a
pretty fairy with shiny dark hair held in place
with a butterfly clip, looks especially sad.

"That's Katie the Kitten Fairy," sighs Crystal, her lovely blue eyes filling with tears. "She's upset because her kitten, Shimmer, has been stolen!"

You pull your dressing gown around you more closely, shivering at the horrible news.

"Who would steal a tiny kitten?" you ask.

The Snow Fairy's voice trails off to a whisper. "It's just the sort of thing that Jack Frost would do! That's why I came to find you. The Pet Keeper Fairies believe that only a girl who truly loves animals will be able to help them find such a precious creature."

You nod your head eagerly, sad to think that a kitten might be caught in the Ice Lord's frosty clutches. Crystal explains that Shimmer is not only adorable, she controls the magic that helps lost and homeless cats find somewhere special to live.

"We should start your adventure with a touch of magic," says your new friend, waving her silvery wand.

Then Crystal asks you to stand in the middle of the room and turn around three times.

* If Crystal sprinkles a fountain of chilly snowflakes above your head, go to 37.
* If the Snow Fairy whispers a magical spell, go to 44.

Queen Titania whispers an ancient spell. Suddenly Jack Frost is there, frozen to the spot!

King Oberon pulls a red velvet cord hanging down from the ceiling. Bertram enters, carrying a purple cushion with a delicate goose egg lying on it, spotted with pretty grey speckles.

"Your birds will return soon," he explains. "And you will also be gaining a larger flock, for the geese are hatching eggs!"

Jack Frost's face lights up when King Oberon explains that the egg on the cushion has been laid by his favourite goose and that the Ice Lord must take good care of it!

A flick of the queen's wand and Jack Frost and his goblins disappear.

You step forward and sadly remind the group that you too must now leave Fairyland.

The queen offers to summon a rainbow for you to ride home on.

"A ride on a rainbow sounds lovely," you smile. "But may I *fly* back to the human world instead? One last flutter with a pair of fairy wings is too exciting to resist!"

The End

It is so cold inside the castle! Jack Frost is slumped on his blue throne, his cape pulled around him.

"Look!" whispers Katie.

Sat at the very top of the throne you see a little fairy! It is Sophia the Snow Swan Fairy, Belle's keeper! Sophia flutters over to greet you.

"Hello," she says in her tiny, tinkly voice. "I'm so sorry to hear about poor Shimmer."

Sophia explains quietly that Jack Frost has lost his pets, too. His entire flock of snowgeese have decided to leave the kingdom! Sophia explains that Jack Frost loved the birds very much. The brave fairy and Belle have come here because even Ice Lords need friendship at times.

Unaware of their presence, Jack Frost shouts out in the echoey chamber.

"If I can't have my pets," he bellows, "why should the Pet Keeper Fairies have theirs?"

You realise that you have to find the geese before Jack Frost kidnaps any more animals!

"We need to move on," you whisper to Katie.

You both hug Sophia, then fly south in search of the geese. Soon you both feel a rush of happiness as the Fairyland Palace rises up before you.

* If you try to get a better view of the palace as you continue your journey south, go to 8.

* If you'd prefer to stop at the royal residence for a brief rest, go to 13.

Cuddling Shimmer in her arms, Katie opens a little arched doorway that winds up to the tallest turret in the Fairyland Palace. As you flutter up and up, you count at least a thousand steps!

"It's breathtaking!" you sigh, taking in the view from the top. All of Fairyland lies stretched out before you. And there, in the distance, you can spot the flock of snowgeese, perched on nests at the far edge of the kingdom.

"Now I understand why the geese left Jack's castle," you say.

Instead of abandoning him, you explain that the birds have flown south, migrating to a warmer place so that they can hatch their eggs!

Just at that moment, you hear a terrible bellowing coming from down below.

Katie's little cheeks pale. "Jack Frost is here!"

From the commotion downstairs, the Ice Lord is clearly hopping mad that Shimmer has been found!

* If you decide to see what the king and queen have to say to the Ice Lord, go to 16.

* If you dash downstairs to explain everything, go to 36.

You and Katie flutter above the grounds of the
Fairyland Palace, hoping against hope that
Shimmer might be near. The stunning rose garden
fanned out beneath you is breathtaking. Although
you know that you should be pressing on with
your search, a funny feeling inside makes you
reluctant to leave.

"Let's go down, Katie," you say. "I think
something strange is happening here."

Even though it's getting late, the Music Fairies
are still busy performing with the king and queen's
frog orchestra. You watch Victoria the Violin Fairy
attempting to try out her solo, but it's very hard to
listen. Her wonderful playing keeps being drowned
out by a dreadful wailing noise. The shrill sound
is out of tune and mournful – not like Victoria's
playing at all.

As you approach, Victoria puts down
her violin, but the wailing keeps
on going! Everyone looks
under their seats, but then
Fiona the Flute Fairy
points to Victoria's violin
case. You rush forwards,
click it open and there's
Shimmer!

★ Turn to the next page! ★

You squeal with sheer delight. The fluffy grey and white kitten tumbles forward into your arms, then curls round your legs in the friendliest greeting imaginable! He gambols through the air, somersaulting with joy until he is reunited with his owner Katie.

"Thank goodness!" laughs the Kitten Fairy, tickling Shimmer's little grey ears.

The kitten's eyes glitter with happiness. Through her purrs, she tells Katie that the goblin who snatched her had been told to hide the cat where a fairy would least expect it — in Fairyland! The hapless intruder spotted Victoria's violin case when he had marched around the back of the palace. It was only when Shimmer started caterwauling to the music that her hiding place was revealed!

Katie is thrilled, but you fear that the fairies' troubles aren't over yet.

"We still need to stop Jack Frost before he tries to snatch any more pets," you warn.

* If you decide to ask the king and queen for help, go to 21.
* If you choose to climb the tallest turret in the palace to see if you can spot Jack Frost's missing snowgeese, go to 29.

"Me-ooww!"

Outside, the tortoiseshell cat starts to mew again.

An excited, bubbly feeling in your heart tells you to push off the window ledge! You flutter your wings and suddenly you're flying over the streets.

"This way Crystal!" you cry. "I think that cat is trying to help us!"

Before you know it, you've travelled so far that the houses have given way to hedgerows and fields.

It's only when you drift down onto a leaf and catch your breath that you realise Crystal the Snow Fairy has disappeared!

Before you can panic, a tiny finger taps you on the shoulder and a little figure appears before you.

"I'm Katie the Kitten Fairy," smiles the fairy. "Crystal had to go back to Fairyland to set the day's weather. But we knew that you would have the courage to come and find me!"

You nod your head shyly.

Katie explains that she has been searching high and low for Shimmer ever since the little cat disappeared, but she still hasn't found a single clue.

As the sun rises, the early morning dewdrops create a lovely rainbow that stretches high above your heads.

* If you decide to flutter up to the top of the rainbow, go to 25.
* If you'd rather ask Katie to lead you to Jack Frost's kingdom, go to 40.

Lara leads you to a quiet spot on the other side of the pond. The little fairy seems to know just where to go! When the coast is clear, Lara explains that Lucky wouldn't rest until she followed you out here. The kind-hearted cat begins to purr, her green eyes glowing with friendship and luck.

"It seems so lonely here," you remark.

Lara nods her head and pulls her blue scarf around her. "Until a few days ago, this pond used to be full of Jack Frost's snowgeese."

Lara explains that the Ice Lord adored the flock, and treated them with great kindness. Then one morning the flock flew off towards the south!

"Jack Frost is boiling with rage," shivers Lara. "Even his favourite snowgoose has left him."

"That explains why he took my Shimmer," cries Katie. "He must be jealous!"

You leap to your feet. To get Shimmer back, you and Katie need to find the missing snowgeese!

You give Lara and Lucky farewell cuddles, before setting off once more. You and Katie take to the skies and fly towards the south.

After a while you spot the magical hillsides of Fairyland in the distance, but there are no snowgeese to be seen.

* If you decide to flutter round to the terraces at the back of the royal palace, go to 13.

* If you decide to go to the palace gardens, go to 30.

Katie asks you to stow away your school things behind the tabby cat family's basket, promising you'll be back in time to finish your project.

"My magic doesn't work so well without Shimmer," says the fairy. "So I'm going to need you to stand as still as a statue."

You stand on the spot as still as can be.

Katie touches her pretty butterfly pendant, then flutters gently above your head. You giggle as a cascade of butterfly sparkles shine down from Katie's wand – fairy dust!

Before the last sparkle fades, something truly magical has happened. You have shrunk to the size of a fairy, and on your back are a pair of gauzy wings, glinting in soft rainbow colours.

"Come on," smiles Katie. "Let's fly around the cattery."

You take Katie's hand and then wriggle your shoulders. Suddenly you're flying high in the air! The cats mew friendly hellos as you flutter over their heads.

Katie darts over to the windowsill.

"Shimmer's definitely not here," she replies. "Are you ready to go somewhere magical?"

* **If you decide to make your way to Jack Frost's Ice Castle, go to 40.**
* **If you'd rather get ready to visit the Pet Keeper Fairies, go to 52.**

You push on past the tortoiseshell cat, swooping down to gently stroke the animal's head. As you flutter past, the cat mews again, but this time you hear something completely different: "Katie's this way! Katie's this way!"

You continue west, and soon pets all over the area call out to you, leading you through the air.

When the first light of morning tinges the sky, Crystal's snowflake necklace starts to glow.

"I need to go to Fairyland," she explains. "It's time for me to help set the weather for the day."

The kind Snow Fairy points to a ginger cat on a fence below you, then waves her wand. The cat will lead you to Katie!

Soon you're fluttering through the morning streets, the cat leaping and running ahead of you.

You flit round one more corner, almost bumping into Katie!

The Kitten Fairy gives you a big hug. She explains that she has been searching all over the human world for Shimmer without any luck at all.

She turns to you, her eyes full of hope. "Where shall we try next?"

Your wings can't help but shudder. All you can think of is Jack Frost and his goblins!

* If you are ready to brave the wilds of Jack Frost's Ice Castle, go to 25.
* If you need a moment to gather your nerves, go to 40.

While the Pet Keeper Fairies stay to search for Shimmer in Fairyland, you and Katie set off. You have set your sights on Jack Frost's Ice Castle!

Within minutes you are flying past the exquisite Fairyland Palace and its delightful formal lawns. When you glide over the rose garden, Katie waves down to the Music Fairies. Poppy the Piano Fairy and her friends are tuning up their instruments, ready to play with the frog orchestra.

"Hello there!" shouts Victoria the Violin Fairy.

The orchestra and the Music Fairies begin a spellbinding waltz, each playing in perfect tune.

As the waltz comes to the middle section, Victoria stands up to perform a violin solo. But when she begins playing, her fiddle is echoed by a terrible screeching sound.

"What's happening?" wonders Katie.

You flap your wings nervously, your eyes roaming the gardens.

* If you decide to move on before any more time is wasted, go to 7.
* If you'd rather glide down and investigate first, go to 30.

You lead the way down to the steps outside the palace ballroom, where Jack Frost is causing the most terrible scene. The Ice Lord's crown glints with menace and ice bolts shoot out of his wand.

You bravely step forward to explain why the geese have flown to warmer climes. When you have finished, Jack Frost is so overwhelmed with relief, he even promises to create a bigger pond for the new baby snowgeese to play in!

"As for you!" he snaps, pointing a bony finger at Katie the Kitten Fairy. "I'm-I'm…well, let's just say no more about it, OK?"

"We'll take that as an apology," decides King Oberon, pointing to the palace doors.

Jack Frost gathers his cloak and an ice bridge appears, transporting him out of the kingdom.

Soon it is time for you to go home, too.

Katie flutters up and gives you a fairy hug.

"From now on you will always have a special connection with animals," she says solemnly. "We will never forget your kindness."

You take to the skies one last time. Everyone cheers and claps in thanks to their honorary fairy friend! As you leave, the sky is filled with a stunning display of fireworks that light up the glittering turrets of the Fairyland Palace.

The End

37

You can't help shivering
a little as you turn three
times on the spot. Above
you, Crystal's wand
pops with a flurry
of snowflakes.

After a few moments,
you feel yourself getting
smaller and smaller.

"You won't need your dressing gown now,"
smiles Crystal. To your surprise, instead of
pyjamas, you are now dressed in a delightful
snow-white dress with floaty sleeves. On your
back you can also feel a pair of filmy fairy wings!

Suddenly you are flying, circling around the
room with Crystal at your side.

It is the most magical sensation in the whole
world! Once you've learnt to flutter your wings
to go higher and to glide slowly back down
again, the Snow Fairy leads you towards the open
window.

"We need to get on our way," urges Crystal.
"We really must track down Shimmer before Jack
Frost and his goblins cause any more trouble!"

* If you decide to dart above the rooftops following the
  calls of the cats, go to 31.

* If you decide to fly up high towards the sparkling moon,
  go to 51.

You run from pen to pen, Katie fluttering at your shoulder. You see black cats, fluffy kittens and elegant Siamese. Each one is delightful, but none of them looks in the least like Shimmer!

You are just about to peer into a pen in the corner, when a mysterious visitor in a hat and raincoat rudely barges past you. Katie hides behind your hair. The frightened fairy points to the bottom of the stranger's coat.

"Look at those ugly green feet," shivers Katie. "It must be a goblin!"

"Where's that fairy?" mutters the stranger. The goblin starts peering into the pens, opening and slamming the doors with bony fingers.

"Oh, my!" gasps Katie. "Jack Frost must have sent him to make sure I don't find Shimmer."

"Shimmer's definitely not here," you whisper. "We'd better press on before any more goblins come after you."

The Pet Keeper Fairy whispers a magical spell into your ear.

Suddenly you find your feet are lifted off the ground in a swoosh of golden glitter!

Katie explains that you'll need to become fairy-sized too to help her find Shimmer!

* If you decide to head straight for Jack Frost's Ice Castle, go to 25.
* If you choose to start your search in Fairyland, go to 42.

Overjoyed by Shimmer's safe discovery, you flutter
up to the rooftop of the Fairyland Palace. You
hope to find the Weather Fairies there.

On the farthest turret you see Doodle, the
weather vane rooster, with seven
gorgeous plumes in his tail.

As soon as you spot the brilliant
blonde locks and fiery dress of Goldie
the Sunshine Fairy, you fly over to
greet her.

"Hello!" you beam, your face
lighting up with excitement

Goldie's warm rays stretch deep
into every corner of Fairyland
and the human world – surely
she'll know where the snowgeese are?

The Sunshine Fairy explains that
the snowgeese haven't deserted Jack Frost, they've
simply flown south to enjoy the warm weather!

"If you come across the Ice Lord," she smiles,
"I suggest you give him this."

Goldie waves her wand and a stunning white
feather appears in your hand.

You take the feather and then flutter away,
wondering what it can mean.

* If you decide to show the feather to the king and queen
  before you present it to Jack Frost, go to 5.

* If you choose to give it to the icy ruler in person, go to 11.

Jack Frost's barren home is the last place in the world that a fairy would want to visit. You pause for a moment, then try and look as brave as you can.

"We don't have any choice, Katie," you decide. "Can you show me the way to Jack Frost's ice kingdom? If he's snatched Shimmer, she could be trapped in his castle."

Katie touches you lightly with her wand. In an instant you feel a delicate silk wrap slide around your shoulders. One appears on the Kitten Fairy too. The sheeny pink wraps are so fine they are almost transparent.

"These will help keep us warm in the snow," she says kindly. "They've been woven by the palace silkworms."

The Pet Keeper Fairy slips her arm through yours, then leads you up towards the clouds. You fly arm-in-arm for hours on end, following the sharp gust of the north wind. Even with the silk wraps, your teeth start to chatter and your little fairy wings begin to tremble.

After a while the grass and flowers beneath you begin to disappear. They are replaced by a layer of frost that soon turns into thick drifts of snow.

You stop for a rest on a thorny branch at the
edge of an eerie icicle forest. Leafless trees dripping
with jewel-like icicles glisten all around.

Ping! Ping! Ping!
A tiny sound echoes through the forest.
"What was that?" asks Katie, her dark eyes
growing wide with concern.

You listen again. It is just the wind whistling
round the icicles, playing the zigzaggy points as
if they were the bars on a giant xylophone.

"Oh dear," sighs your friend. "I don't think
Shimmer would like it here at all."

* If you decide to fly on towards Jack Frost's Ice Castle, go to 41.
* If you decide to explore the icicle forest first, go to 50.

You fly even deeper into Jack Frost's frozen world.
Snow and ice stretch as far as the eye can see.
It truly is the most cold and unwelcoming place
you've ever found yourself in.

"I don't like it here," says Katie. "Let's hurry."

The Pet Keeper Fairy sprinkles some golden
fairy dust over your head. Suddenly your rainbow
wings are lifted by a rush of warm air. You both
soar over a steep mountain peak, flitting past
icy crevasses and lonely stone passes. When you
emerge on the other side, the sight before you is
enough to make you tremble.

There, in the distance, is Jack Frost's castle, a
pointy blue building hewn from ancient ice. Its
sharp turrets and barred doorway look ominous
and forbidding.

"Let's hide here for a moment," says Katie,
leading you to the shelter of a frozen pond.

You suggest trying to flutter in through a
window, but before Katie can reply you feel bony
green hands grab you roughly by the shoulders.
You turn round to see eight ugly goblins grinning
from ear to ear.

"What you doin' here, Miss?" cackles one. "Jack
Frost's gonna be very interested indeed!"

"Let go of me!" you cry.

While one goblin reaches for a piece of rope tied to his belt, another makes a swipe at Katie.

"You're Shimmer's keeper, ain't you?" he grunts, his eyes wide with delight.

"We haven't got time to waste with you goblins," Katie answers proudly. "Take that!"

Katie reaches forward and tweaks his nose. Before the creature can lurch for her again, the agile little fairy manages to somersault out of his grasp.

"Katie!" you yell, pointing. The Kitten Fairy's precious wand is tumbling out of her hand!

* If you try to catch the golden wand, go to 9.
* If you decide to wriggle until the goblin lets go of your wings, go to 43.

You flutter into the air and take Katie's hands. The Kitten Fairy whispers a wishing spell that makes your wings flutter in its magical breeze.

You open your eyes just as your toes touch down on the greenest grass you have ever seen.

Katie's cheeks break into happy dimples. "Welcome to Fairyland!"

Katie leads you into a pretty valley full of red-topped toadstool houses. The Pet Keeper Fairies' house is easy to find. It has a neat garden filled with hutches, with a small stable at the end.

As soon as you reach the door, Bella, Georgia and Harriet run out to greet you both.

"We've been looking everywhere for Shimmer," sighs Bella, fluttering her shiny green wings.

Before you know it, all of the Pet Keeper Fairies apart from Penny are standing in a circle around you. The friends tell you that they were all in bed when the kitten was taken.

"I'm going to take a look around," you say. "There might be a clue here that could lead us to Shimmer."

* If you decide to explore the garden, go to 45.
* If you'd rather look around the fairies' bedroom, go to 56.

You wriggle around, determined to free yourself from the goblin's tight clutches. As Katie's wand tumbles to the ground, its tip brushes your wings.

"Owww!" bellows the goblin. The meanie instantly lets go of you, shouting that your wings have grown too hot to touch!

You look at Katie and smile, grateful for her fairy magic.

Jumpy and confused by the fairy magic, the pack of goblins run back to their Ice Castle home.

You flutter forward and give Katie a hug.

"Your wand certainly showed them a thing or two about fairy magic!" you grin. "Thank you."

Before you can swoop down to search on the floor for the golden wand, a stunning fairy with glossy black hair taps you on the shoulder.

"Is this what you're looking for?" she smiles, holding the wand in her fingertips.

"Lara!" says Katie, her face lighting up. The Pet Keeper Fairy gives the stranger a hug, then bends down to stroke the tiny cat that is perched in Lara's arms.

"I'm the Black Cat Fairy," smiles Lara, turning to you. "And this magical animal is called Lucky."

* If you decide to find out what Lara is doing in this desolate land, go to 17.
* If you'd rather fly on together until the goblins are completely out of sight, go to 32.

You follow Crystal's instructions to the letter, fizzing with anticipation. As you turn on the spot, you shut your eyes tight. In the background you hear the chime of Crystal's sweet voice.

"*Human friend, so kind and true,*" she whispers. "*Let Rainbow Magic transform you!*"

You feel a gentle tap on your back as the fairy touches you with her wand. When you open your eyes, you're in for an enchanting surprise.

You've shrunk to tiny proportions and a pair of delicate wings have grown on your back!

"I-I-I can fly?" you gasp.

Crystal giggles and flutters into the glow of a moonbeam, then shows you how to twist and turn in the air.

The kind fairy lets you practise for a minute or two before leading you out towards the open window. One after the other, you gracefully glide down and then perch on the nearest streetlight. On the pavement below, the cat you'd seen earlier is still mewing into the night air.

"Poor Shimmer could be anywhere by now," says Crystal. "We have to find him!"

* If you choose to head west past the tortoiseshell cat, go to 34.
* If you decide to make your way east towards the far horizon, go to 55.

You find yourself in the Pet Keeper Fairies' garden, searching for clues.

Apart from some of Shimmer's favourite kitten toys scattered on the grass, there is nothing to help you work out where she might have gone.

Just then, Penny the Pony Fairy canters up on Glitter. She has been riding all over the kingdom, searching for Shimmer. As soon as she sees you, Penny trots over to say hello.

"I have some information!" she cries, her pretty blue eyes sparkling with excitement.

Penny tells you that she bumped into a goblin at the far edge of Fairyland.

"I tricked him into telling me that Jack Frost's snowgeese have flown away," she explains. "Even his favourite snowgoose has left!"

"That must be why he snatched Shimmer," suggests Harriet the Hamster Fairy.

You nod your head. "Jack Frost must have stolen Shimmer out of pure jealousy!"

* **If you decide to go the Fairyland Palace and report Penny's news to King Oberon and Queen Titania, go to 15.**

* **If you decide to stay in the garden with the Pet Keeper Fairies, go to 48.**

You sit quietly, using your A4 file to hide Katie from the other children until everybody has left the room. As soon as the cattery is empty again, Katie begins to wave her golden wand.

"If you're truly going to help," she smiles, "you'll need a touch of fairy magic."

You gasp as you feel yourself being lifted off the ground, rising upwards until your feet no longer touch the floor!

Within seconds you find yourself hovering in midair next to Katie, her face beaming with a sweet fairy smile. You've shrunk to the size of a fairy!

"Fly up to the ceiling," urges Katie, reaching for your hand.

The fairy points to your delicate pair of rainbow wings. You're a natural flyer – a few flutters and practice loop-the-loops and you're ready to start your search!

"Shimmer's definitely not here," you decide. "Perhaps we should go back to the place where you saw her last?"

Katie squeezes through a gap in the window, then beckons for you to follow. "Let's hurry. We need to get you back in time to finish off your schoolwork."

* **If you decide to hold Katie's hand and shut your eyes tight, go to 42.**
* **If you'd prefer to fly up towards the rainbow that you can see shining through the window, go to 52.**

The alarm wakes you from a deep sleep. You stretch and rub your eyes.

Did you really meet a Weather Fairy last night? The memory of Crystal the Snow Fairy shimmering on your windowsill is so magical, you wonder if it could have been a dream. Even so, you hurry to get dressed as fast as you can, determined to be ready in case the Rainbow Magic fairies really do need your help.

On your way to school, you remember that you are going on a trip this morning! Your teacher has arranged for your class to visit a local animal rescue centre. This half term you've been working on a brilliant project all about pets.

When you arrive, the Centre Manager, Sally, gives you a tour round the building, introducing all the animals that are waiting to be re-homed.

⭐ Turn to the next page! ⭐

When Sally leads your group into the cattery, her face falls. The room is packed with cats and kittens – adorable creatures each looking hopefully up at you.

"I can't understand why we have so many cats in the centre right now," she sighs. "Nobody's come in for days."

Sally explains to your teacher that unless some families come in to volunteer a new home soon, she might have to close the doors to new kittens and cats. While the adults talk, you and your friends bend down to stroke the gorgeous cats curled up in each of the pens.

"Look at this one!" you cry, pointing to a friendly-faced tabby.

The cat is nursing four sweet little kittens. Two are striped, one is sandy brown and one is pure white. You listen to their contented purring, then bend closer – through the cats' quiet mews you are sure you heard the words "Please help us!"

* If you decide to search for clues in the pen, go to 23.
* If you choose to whisper back to the kittens, go to 49.

"If you are going to help me take on Jack Frost and his goblins," says Katie, "you'll need an extra-strong boost of fairy magic."

Lauren the Puppy Fairy nods her head. "Time to form a fairy ring."

The seven friends lead you to a shady corner at the bottom of their garden. The fairies stand you in the middle of the lawn and then form a ring of hands around you.

"Ready everybody?" asks Katie. "Let's join wands!"

You watch as the fairies each raise their wands, sending a fountain of magical sparkles fizzing over your head. The six pets gambol in midair above you all. You are amazed to discover that you can understand every sound they utter!

You look back at your wings. Already you feel much stronger.

By the time the kind fairies put down their wands, you feel ready to seek out Jack Frost. It's time to get Shimmer back where she belongs!

* If you suggest that Katie flies with you towards the Fairyland Palace, go to 18.
* If you ask the Pet Keeper Fairies to show you the direction of Jack Frost's ice kingdom, go to 35.

"What can I do?" you whisper. You have no idea what might be happening, but you feel sure that it has something to do with Rainbow Magic!

The mother cat looks up and begins to mew gently. You can understand what she is saying!

"Please help us. Shimmer is lost!"

Suddenly, a group of golden butterflies flutter out of the cats' basket! You peer inside.

"Shimmer is my kitten!" chimes a tiny voice. A tiny fairy darts into the air!

"I'm Katie the Kitten Fairy!" smiles the little fairy.

Katie explains that she is a Pet Keeper Fairy, one of seven friends who use their magic to look after all animals.

"Shimmer was stolen from Fairyland last night," she cries. "I'm sure that Jack Frost has got her!"

"Can I have your attention please, everyone?" booms a voice from the other side of the room.

The teacher tells you that you have the rest of the day as free time to explore the centre and work on your projects.

As the other pupils head off in all directions, you reach in to comfort Katie.

"I'll help you find Shimmer," you whisper gently. "I promise."

* If you choose to start searching for Shimmer right away, go to 38.
* If you think it's safer to hide in the pen until you're sure that the coast is clear, go to 46.

You summon all your courage and make your way to the shivery icicle forest. The trees cast strange shadows on the snow. As you and Katie dart left and right through the trees, you can't help feeling colder and colder.

"Let's stop for a moment," says Katie, her little arms dotted with goosebumps.

The Kitten Fairy sprinkles fairy dust over you both. Your eyes shine with wonder as a thousand golden butterflies glitter in the icy air. Suddenly, you are filled with magical warm tingles from head to toe!

"Thank you," you smile. "That's much better."

You join hands and flutter on. You pass spiky trees and lonely valleys covered in thick snow. Katie puts her finger to her lips, telling you to whisper.

"This place is dangerous," she warns. "If we make too much noise, we could start an avalanche."

After a while you reach a clearing, the site of a frozen pond. Perched elegantly in the middle is a petite white swan.

"That's a magical animal!" gasps Katie. "She belongs to my friend, Sophia the Snow Swan Fairy!"

Turn to the next page!

"Perhaps she can help us?" you suggest.

"Belle!" Katie calls gently. "Is that you?"

There is a moment of serene silence before the beautiful swan arches its curved neck in acknowledgement. Belle flaps her wings and calls back to you both. When her little beak moves, it almost seems as if the bird is smiling!

"She's saying that she wants us to stay near this pond," says Katie.

Your wings flutter nervously. Shouldn't you be pressing on after Shimmer?

* **If you choose to flutter over the frozen pond to greet Belle, go to 2.**
* **If you ask the swan to come with you as you flutter deeper into the forest, go to 54.**

You push away from the window ledge, then spiral upwards. The magical moonbeams bathe you in silver light.

The light soon gets so bright, you both have to close your eyes whilst you continue to fly. When you open them again the moon has given way to the first sunbeams of morning.

You blink and rub your eyes when you see that not one but two fairies are now fluttering alongside you! Your new companion has beautiful pink-tinged wings. You know at once that she must be Katie the Kitten Fairy!

"Hello," smiles Katie.

Crystal greets Katie and then looks up at the golden sunrise. "Now you've found Katie, I must get back to Fairyland. I need to help set the day's weather before everyone wakes up!"

You and Katie wave goodbye. When the Snow Fairy has gone, your companion turns to you and clutches both of your hands.

"I think we should go to Fairyland too," she says, her eyes twinkling with excitement.

Katie is sure that her kingdom holds the clue to Shimmer's whereabouts, if only she could decide where to start...

*   If you ask Katie to take you to meet the rest of the Pet Keeper Fairies, go to 42.
*   If you lead your new friend towards the distant rainbow that you can see curving across the sunrise, go to 52.

You stretch your wings and then flutter up as fast as you can, holding tightly on to Katie's hand. Behind you a trail of gold fairy dust sparkles in the light.

Up above, you can see a stunning rainbow stretching across the land. Remembering that these colourful archways only appear when it is sunny and rainy at the same time, you notice that there isn't a raindrop to be seen for miles around.

Katie giggles and nods. "This is a magic rainbow. Fairies can slide down it."

The Kitten Fairy leads you up through white clouds that are so puffy you can jump on them as if they were trampolines. Finally you reach the top of the magical arch. You sit at the top of the rainbow, then push yourself down.

You are sure the colourful slide is going to lead you to Fairyland and the Pet Keeper Fairies' home, but as you glide down you can suddenly hear voices calling through the breeze.

"Katie! Katie!" shout the voices. "Is that you?"

The Kitten Fairy points down towards the bottom of the rainbow.

"It's Kirsty and Rachel!" she gasps, her eyes as wide as saucers. "Let's make a quick stop. They might have some news about Shimmer."

Katie pulls you off the rainbow so fast you are both sent tumbling through the sky. You land with a bump on the beach on Rainspell Island!

"Oops, sorry!" says Katie.

Rachel Walker and Kirsty Tate rush to greet you. They are both bursting with questions.

"Do you know where Shimmer is?" asks Rachel.

Kirsty looks worried. "Has mean Jack Frost taken her?"

The girls explain that they realised something was wrong when the little kitten gem on their lovely pet charm bracelets disappeared. The best friends were given the bracelets by Queen Titania when they helped the Pet Keeper Fairies during a half-term holiday.

"We've been searching all day," sighs Rachel. "But Shimmer definitely isn't hiding here."

Katie thanks the girls then waves her wand – you need to get to Fairyland straightaway!

* If you find yourself whisked into the Pet Keeper Fairies' garden, go to 45.
* If you arrive in a shimmer of fairy dust in Katie's bedroom, go to 56.

You flutter down the stairs of the toadstool house, followed by Katie, Harriet and the rest of the Pet Keeper Fairies. In the distance you can see Jack Frost's snowgeese flying into the horizon in a beautiful triangle formation.

"Come on, Katie!" you cry. "Let's follow those birds."

You flutter up after the geese, determined to find out where they might be going. If you can get his pets back, maybe there's a chance that Jack Frost will show you where he's hidden poor Shimmer!

You soon realise that the geese are flying so fast, it's difficult for your tiny fairy wings to keep up.

By the time the snowgeese have disappeared out of sight, you find yourselves gliding above the Fairyland Palace swimming pool.

Down below, Samantha the Swimming Fairy pulls off her pink goggles and calls up to you, her lovely black hair glistening with water. She is pointing to a strange character floating on a lilo, dressed in shades and a wetsuit.

* If you decide to flutter over to the mystery stranger, go to 3.
* If you decide to stop and speak to Samantha, go to 19.

You explain to Belle that you don't have time to stay in the forest. You tell her the news of Shimmer's disappearance.

"Will you fly with us?" you ask. "We need to find Jack Frost's Ice Castle."

The swan nods her elegant neck.

As you travel over the icicle forest, Katie reminds you that Belle has the power to spread compassion and kindness throughout Fairyland and the human world. Could there be someone here who needs her help?

Katie suddenly remembers that Jack Frost's flock of snowgeese normally swim on the frozen pond!

"The geese are his pets," she explains. "I wonder where they have gone?"

You can't help but feel a little sorry for the Ice Lord. He must be missing the geese terribly!

Suddenly, the Ice Castle looms up before you, and you hear a sing-song fairy voice calling Belle's name. The swan glides in through a balcony window. You follow, your wings shaking with excitement.

"Oh, Katie!" you tremble.

You realise you are in Jack Frost's throne room... and the Ice Lord himself is there!

* If you decide to dart behind the throne before Jack Frost can see you, go to 6.
* If you decide to seek out the fairy who called for Belle, go to 28.

You peer out into the starry darkness.

"Let's go this way!" you cry, pointing east.

You both flutter out into the night air and fly for hours, always keeping an eye out for Shimmer.

"She's got brilliant green eyes and fluffy white and grey fur," explains Crystal. "In the human world, Shimmer can grow big or shrink down to fairy-size whenever she likes."

Finally the Snow Fairy reaches for your hand and leads you down to a field, where Katie the Kitten Fairy is waiting to meet you. The little fairy is surrounded by a group of animals.

"Oh, hello!" smiles Katie. "I was just asking these animals if they'd seen Shimmer."

The Pet Keeper Fairy tells you that she's spent all night searching the human world with no luck.

"Shall we try somewhere else?" you suggest.

Katie nods enthusiastically.

"I'll keep looking round here," says Crystal. "Good luck, you two!"

* If you and Katie decide to take your search to Jack Frost's ice kingdom, go to 40.
* If you choose to close your eyes and let Katie's magic whisk you to Fairyland, go to 42.

In no time you are standing in the delightful
bedroom that Katie the Kitten Fairy shares with
her six best friends. Lauren the Puppy Fairy shows
you where each of them sleep, in cosy beds draped
with gauzy curtains and a special bed for each of
their beloved animals.

Molly the Goldfish Fairy's auburn curls tumble
and shine as she shows you the little bedtime
bowl she has for her fish, Flash. Penny the Pony
Fairy runs through the door leading Glitter. In
Fairyland, magical ponies are allowed to sleep
with their fairy owners too!

★ Turn to the next page! ★

"There's Shimmer's basket," sighs Katie, pointing to a tiny wicker crib in the corner.

You run up to the empty basket and take a close look inside. There's nothing to see apart from a fluffy pink blanket, until you glance down at the floor. On the edge of the fairies' neat polka-dot rug is a large ugly footprint! The prints lead across the rug and out of the toadstool door.

"Whoever made these footprints was big, chubby-toed and extremely muddy," you announce.

There is only one possible culprit – a goblin!

Bella the Bunny Fairy gives her pet Misty a protective cuddle, trembling at the thought of an intruder creeping into their bedroom.

While you ask why Jack Frost would have sent his goblins to do such a mean thing, Georgia looks out of the window and gasps! There, winging their way overhead, is Jack Frost's beloved flock of snowgeese.

"Oh, my!" cries Harriet the Hamster Fairy. "Even the Ice Lord's favourite goose is there, right in the middle of the group."

"It looks like they're heading south," adds Molly, fluttering up to the window pane.

Katie's eyes sparkle. "So that's why Jack Frost is angry with the Pet Keeper Fairies. He's just bitter because his own pets have abandoned him!"

* If you choose to follow the trail of goblin footprints, go to 4.
* If you think it's better to run out of the toadstool cottage and flutter after the geese, go to 53.

If you liked this story
you'll love these other fantastic
Rainbow Magic books!

Ruby the Red Fairy
Choose Your Own Magic
978-1-40830-789-2

Juliet the Valentine Fairy
978-1-40831-135-6

Look out for the Ocean Fairies!

ALLY THE DOLPHIN FAIRY
978-1-40830-815-8

AMELIE THE SEAL FAIRY
978-1-40830-816-5

PIA THE PENGUIN FAIRY
978-1-40830-817-2

TESS THE SEA TURTLE FAIRY
978-1-40830-818-9

STEPHANIE THE STARFISH FAIRY
978-1-40830-819-6

WHITNEY THE WHALE FAIRY
978-1-40830-820-2

COURTNEY THE CLOWNFISH FAIRY
978-1-40830-821-9

Available April 2010

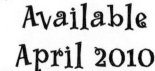